Thank You
for a
Wonderful Year!

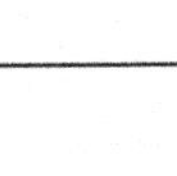

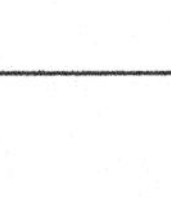

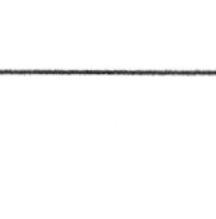

Made in the USA
Monee, IL
24 November 2021

82942633R00063